A BOY, A DOG
and A FROG

by Mercer Mayer

DIAL BOOKS FOR YOUNG READERS
New York

To my family,
Marianna and Samantha

Published by Dial Books for Young Readers
A division of Penguin Books USA Inc.
375 Hudson Street, New York, New York 10014
Copyright © 1967 by Mercer Mayer. All rights reserved.
Library of Congress Catalog Card Number: 67-22254
Printed in Hong Kong by South China Printing Co.
COBE
14 16 18 20 19 17 15

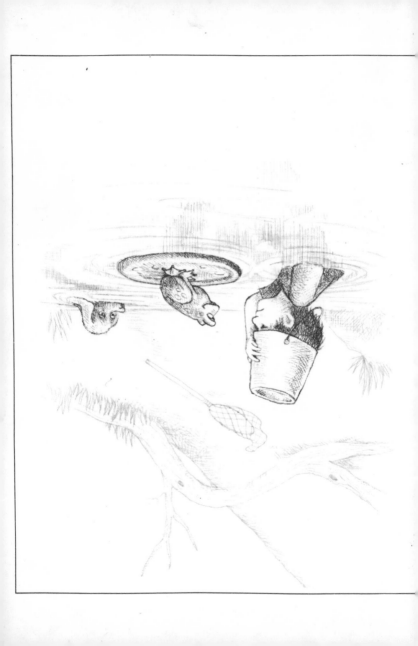

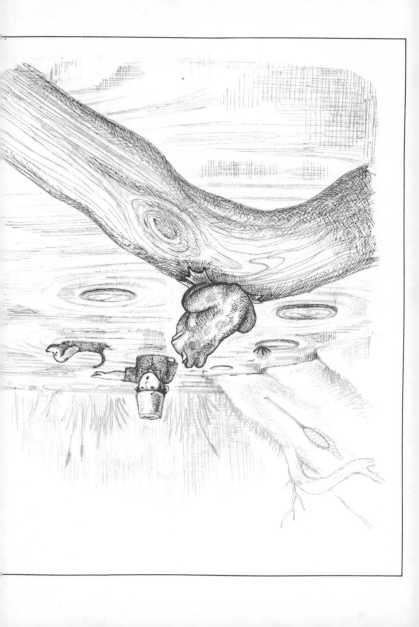

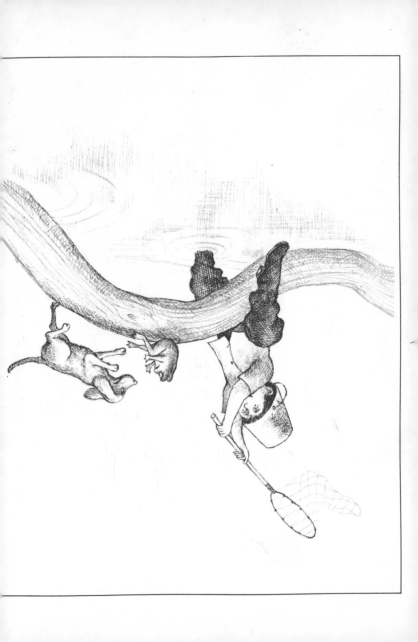

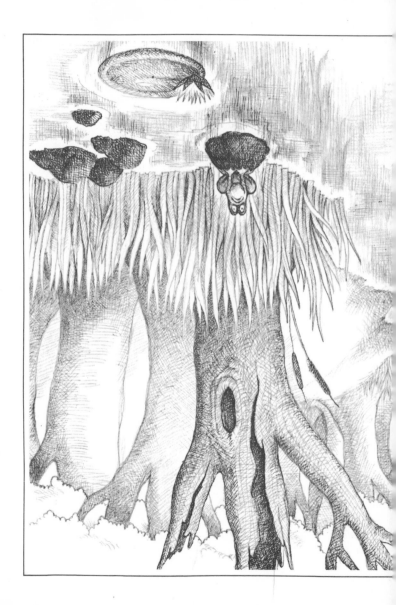

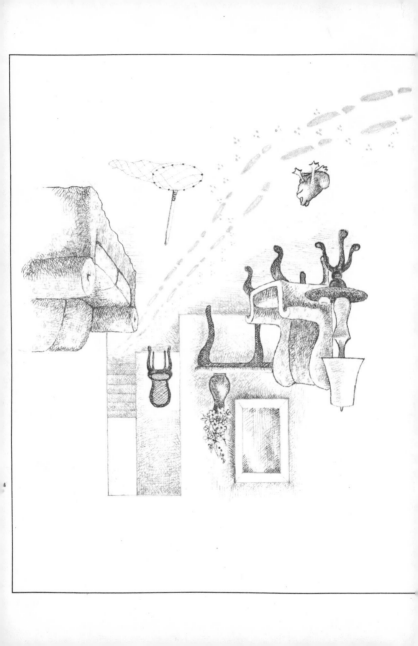

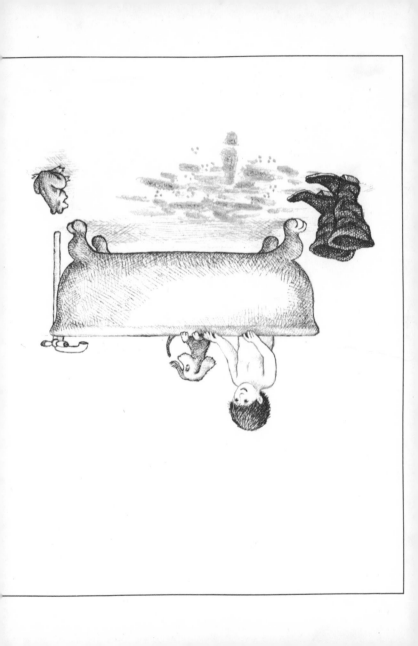

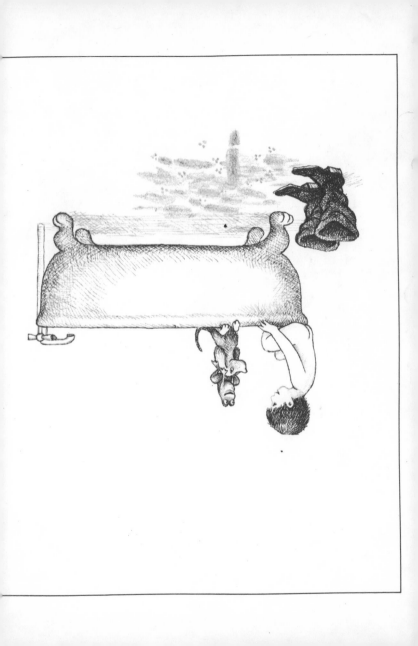